DATE DUE		

Times Tables Cheat

by Anastasia Suen
illustrated by Jeff Ebbeler

Content Consultant:
Vicki F. Panaccione, Ph.D.
Licensed Child Psychologist
Founder, Better Parenting Institute

visit us at
www.abdopublishing.com

Printed in the United States.

Text by Anastasia Suen
Illustrations by Jeff Ebbeler
Edited by Patricia Stockland
Interior layout and design by Becky Daum
Cover design by Becky Daum

Library of Congress Cataloging-in-Publication Data

Suen, Anastasia.
  Times tables cheat / Anastasia Suen ; illustrated by Jeffery Ebbeler.
    p. cm. — (Main Street school)
  Summary: When he refuses to help Dalton cheat on his multiplication test, Alex then suggests they study together, helping each other with their weak subjects.
  ISBN 978-1-60270-034-5
  [1. Cheating—Fiction. 2. Cooperativness—Fiction. 3. Friendship—Fiction. 4. Schools—Fiction.] I. Ebbeler, Jeffrey, ill. II. Title.

  PZ7.S94343Ti 2007
  [E]—dc22
                                        2007004724

Pur 4/09

Alex sat behind Isaiah on the bus.

"I know all my threes," said Alex.
"Do not," said Isaiah.

"Do so," said Alex.
"3, 6, 9, 12, 15, 18, 21, 24,
27, 30, 33, 36!"

3

"Okay," said Isaiah. "But do you know your fours?"

"Sure," said Alex. "4, 8, 12 . . ."

"What is with you two?" asked Dalton. *Click! Click! Click!* He didn't look up from his handheld game.

Alex turned to look at Dalton. "We're practicing our times tables."

"I know that," said Dalton. "But we're not in school yet."

"What if we have a pop quiz?" asked Alex.

"Miss K doesn't give one every day,"
said Dalton. His thumbs kept moving
on the game.

"That's just it," said Isaiah. "You never
know when it's coming."

Click! Click! "Yes!" said Dalton.
"I've reached Level 14!"

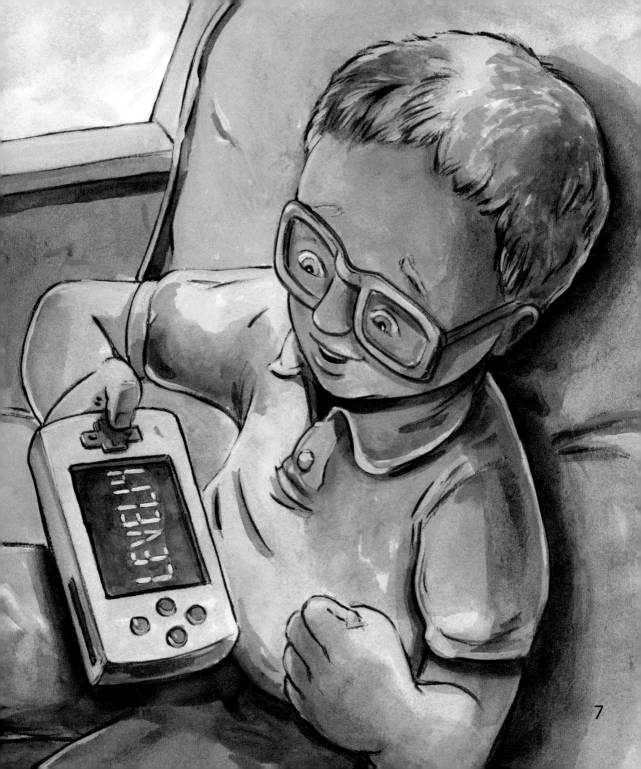

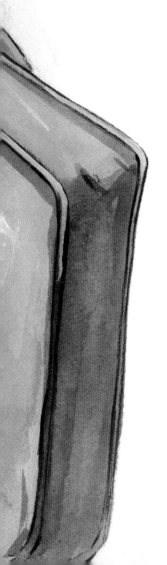

"How did you get so high?" asked Alex. "I'm only on Level 3."

"Practice," said Dalton.
Click! Click! Click!

Isaiah leaned over the seat and pointed at the screen. "What is that?"

"I found it in Level 5," said Dalton. "Watch this!" *Click! Click! Click!*

"I didn't know you could do that," said Alex.

The bus stopped. Alex stood up and put on his backpack. So did Isaiah.

"We're here already?" asked Dalton. *Click! Click! Click!* His thumbs kept moving on the game. "I haven't finished this level!"

"If Miss K sees that game . . ." said Isaiah.

"I know, I know," said Dalton.
"I'm putting it away." He put the
game in his backpack.

"You can play on the way home,"
said Alex.

"That won't be for hours," said
Dalton. He followed Isaiah and
Alex off the bus.

"Pop quiz!" said Miss K when math started.
"I want to see if you know your times tables."

Alex looked at Isaiah. "I hope she does
the threes."

"Me, too," said Isaiah.

"Are you ready?" asked Miss K.

"Wait," said Dalton. "Alex, can I borrow a
sheet of paper?"

"You need to be more prepared," said Miss K.

"Yes, Miss K," said Dalton.

Alex reached into his desk. He pulled out a sheet of paper. "Here you go."

"Thanks," said Dalton.

"Now," said Miss K, "write out your sevens."

Alex started writing.

Psst . . . psst!

What was that noise? Alex looked up. Dalton was looking at Alex.

What is this, thought Alex. *Does he want me to give him the answer?*

Dalton pointed at his paper. Then he put six fingers in the air.

Six, thought Alex. *He must not know 7 times 6.*

Alex looked down at his paper. He wondered why Dalton wanted him to cheat.

If Miss K finds out, she'll give both of us an F! he thought. Alex wanted to be a good friend, but he didn't want to cheat.

Psst . . . psst!

Alex tried to ignore Dalton. Then Miss K walked over. She stood next to Alex.

"I'm not doing anything wrong!" said Alex.

Alex quickly wrote the rest of his sevens.

"Time's up," said Miss K.

Dalton groaned.

"Trade with your partner," said Miss K.

Alex traded papers with Dalton.

"Let's say the sevens aloud," said Miss K as she walked around the room.

As the class said the sevens, Alex marked Dalton's paper. X, X, X, X, X . . .

Dalton doesn't know his sevens, thought Alex. *They're not that hard.*

"Write the number of correct answers at the top," said Miss K. Alex wrote a 3 at the top of Dalton's paper.

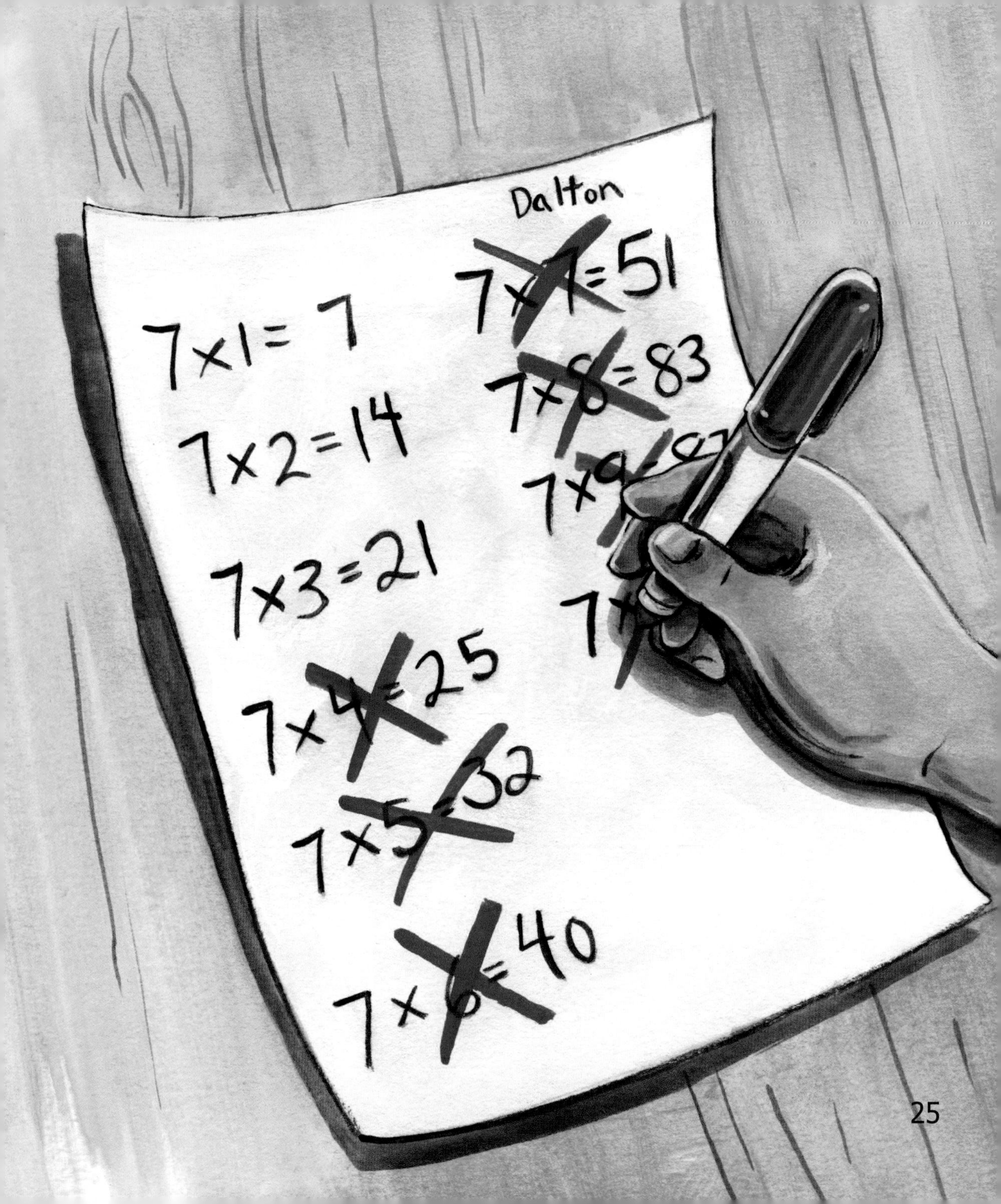
Dalton
7×1= 7
7×2=14
7×3=21
7×4=25
7×5=32
7×6=40
7×7=51
7×8=83

Alex gave Dalton his quiz. "I only got three right?" asked Dalton. "That stinks! Why didn't you help me?"

"Miss K was standing there," said Alex. "Besides, I didn't want an F. Cheating isn't honest."

"Some friend you are," said Dalton.

"You don't have to cheat," said Alex.

"But I didn't know the answers," said Dalton.

"That's because you didn't practice," said Alex.

"The sevens are just football scores," said Alex. "7, 14, 21 . . ."

"I got those three," said Dalton. "It's the other ones I didn't know."

"You can practice with us," said Alex.

Dalton looked at his paper. "Okay, okay, but not on the way home. I have to play my game, too."

"Can you help me get to Level 4?" asked Alex.

"Sure," said Dalton. "It just takes practice."

What Do You Think?

1. Why didn't Dalton want to practice his times tables on the bus?

2. How did Dalton get to Level 14 in his game?

3. Why did Dalton try to cheat?

4. Do you think Alex should have told Dalton the answer?

Words to Know

cheat—to act dishonestly in order to win a game or get what you want.
friend—someone whom you enjoy being with.
honest—being truthful and not lying or stealing or cheating.
pressure—strong influence, force, or persuasion.
temptation—something that you want to have or do, although you know it is wrong.

Miss K's Classroom Rules

1. Ask for help if you don't understand what the teacher is saying.
2. Make time to study.
3. Do your own work. Putting your name on someone else's work is cheating, too.
4. Don't give your work to someone else.

31

Web Sites

To learn more about honesty, visit ABDO Publishing Company on the World Wide Web at **www.abdopublishing.com**. Web sites about honesty are featured on our Book Links page. These links are routinely monitored and updated to provide the most current information available.